At Home
by the Ocean

Sharon Gordon

Marshall Cavendish
Benchmark
New York

Come see my home.

I live by the ocean.

Can you feel the sea breeze?

Taste the salty air.

I walk on the beach with my family.

We find beautiful shells.

The hills of sand are called *dunes*.

They keep houses safe from wind and waves.

We cover our windows
before a big storm.

We leave the beach in
a *hurricane*.

We have a fishing boat.

We go out early in the morning.

We are dirty after a day in the wind and sand.

It helps to have a shower outside!

The tall *lighthouse* helps boats at night.

They look for its bright light.

In the winter, the beach is quiet.

But in the summer, it is very busy.

People come to swim and surf.

We see old friends again.

Flags show when it is safe to go in the water.

Lifeguards watch for swimmers in trouble.

Now the beach is wide.

The *tide* is low.

But high tide is coming.

Watch out for the waves!

Ocean Home

beach

boat

dunes

lifeguard

lighthouse

Challenge Words

dunes (DOONS) Hills of sand that have been built by the wind.

hurricane (HUR-i-kane) A storm with strong winds and heavy rain.

lighthouse (LIGHT-house) A tower with a bright light on top to guide ships.

tide (TIDE) The rise and fall of the water in the ocean.

29

Index

Page numbers in **boldface** are illustrations.

About the Author

Sharon Gordon has written many books for young children. She has always worked as an editor. Sharon and her husband Bruce have three children, Douglas, Katie, and Laura, and one spoiled pooch, Samantha. They live in Midland Park, New Jersey.

With thanks to Nanci Vargus, Ed.D. and
Beth Walker Gambro, reading consultants

Marshall Cavendish Benchmark
Marshall Cavendish
99 White Plains Road
Tarrytown, New York 10591-9001
www.marshallcavendish.us

Library of Congress Cataloging-in-Publication Data

Gordon, Sharon.
At home by the ocean / by Sharon Gordon.
p. cm. — (Bookworms. At home)
Includes index.
Summary: "Describes life by the ocean, including dunes, hurricanes, lighthouses,
and tides"—Provided by publisher.
ISBN 0-7614-1959-4
1. Ocean—Juvenile literature. 2. Oceanography—Juvenile literature. I. Title.
GC21.5.G67 2005
551.45'7—dc22
2004025383

Photo Research by Anne Burns Images

Cover Photo by *Corbis*/Bob Krist

The photographs in this book are used with permission and through the courtesy of:
Corbis: pp. 1, 9, 28 (lower) Macduff Everton; p. 3 Catherine Karnow; p. 5 Kim Robbie;
p. 7 John Henry; pp. 13, 28 (upper r.) Forest Johnson; p. 17, 29 (right) Roger Ball;
pp. 19, 28 (upper l.) Kelly/Mooney Photography; p. 21 LWA-Dann Tardif;
pp. 23, 29 (left) David H. Wells; p. 25 Bob Krist; p. 27 Karen Huntt. *Photri-Microstock*: p. 11.
Index Stock Imagery: p. 15 Terri Froelich.

Series design by Becky Terhune

Printed in Malaysia
1 3 5 6 4 2